INSIDE AT THE SEASIDE

Patricia Orelaja

This book is dedicated to my beloved children;
Sheree, KK & Temi

Temi and KK were so excited. The day had finally arrived for their trip to the seaside with Mum.

Everything was perfect: the sun was shining, and the bags were all packed and ready to go. All they had to do was to wait patiently for their taxi to arrive.

"Stop running around!" demanded Mum, "It won't be too long now. Why don't you go and look out of the window and see who can spot the taxi first?"

They both stood at the window pressing their hands and faces right up against the warm glass.

"I am so excited," shouted Temi. "I am looking forward the most to a tall, whippy ice-cream with sprinkles, red and chocolate sauce and a big chocolate flake sticking out of the side."

All of a sudden, the sky went dark, the sun seemed to disappear and hide behind the tree opposite their house.

Then, there was a noise at the window, only very feint at first.

Then there was a trickle,
then a patter,
then a pitter patter.

"RAIN!" screamed Temi.

Temi threw herself onto the floor. She cried almost as much as the raindrops outside.

"It's not fair, now we can't go to the seaside," wailed Temi.

"I know, I have a good idea," said KK. "Why don't we pretend that we are at the seaside?"

"NO!" answered Temi angrily. Then she paused and sheepishly asked, "What do you mean?"

"Let's start with the sand." KK took out a bright yellow blanket from the toy box and laid it out on the floor.

"That's not sand," said Temi looking confused.

KK then dragged over their two deckchairs from the front door. He put them side-by-side on the rug.

Temi's face lit up… just a little.

"What about the sea?" demanded Temi. "You can't have the seaside without the sea!"

"Well," said KK, "I have a great idea. Let's get two bowls and fill them with warm water. We can put them in front of our deckchairs and pretend that we are wading our feet in the sea."

Temi's face lit up… this time a lot more.

"It almost feels like the seaside, but what about the seagulls? There are always seagulls at the seaside, aren't there?"

"Well," said KK, "I have a great idea. Let's get some sounds from the iPad. Let's type in seagull sounds."

In a few seconds, the room was filled with the sound of seagulls and crashing waves.

So now they had the sand, the sea, the noise of the seaside and deckchairs. What more could they want?

"What about the donkey rides? We always have them when we visit the seaside," muttered Temi.

"Well," said KK, "I have a great idea." He went to get Mum's brown coat.

He laid it over his back, got onto his hands and knees and beamed, "Your donkey awaits."

Temi got on his back and she laughed and laughed with her hands up in the air. This was the best donkey ride she had ever had.

"KK this is perfect…well almost. If only I could have my big whippy ice-cream with sprinkles, red and chocolate sauce and a big chocolate flake sticking out of the side."

She paused thoughtfully and said… "But thank you KK."

They both sat happily stretched out on their deckchairs with their feet in the water, talking and listening to the sounds of the seaside and just having a thoroughly great time.

Tcmi and KK had been so busy having fun that they didn't realise that the rain had stopped and the sun was peeping back through the window.

They were enjoying themselves so much that the seaside sounds from the iPad drowned out even the sounds of the ice-cream van outside.

Dad finally arrived home at the end of the day. Can you guess what he had in his hands?

Yes, two big whippy ice-creams with sprinkles, red and chocolate sauce and a big chocolate flake sticking out of the side.

Temi and KK both sat back in their deckchairs, splashing their feet in the water with their sun hats and glasses on with the sun now shining through the window and an ice-cream in their hands.

The day hadn't quite gone as planned, but they had a fantastic day.

It was like being...
INSIDE AT THE SEASIDE.

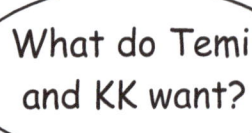

To download a full 'Original lesson plan & resource guide'
please visit our website **www.ppmevents.com** or write to:

Pixel Power Media,
85a Elmers End Road,
Beckenham, Kent BR3 4SY

www.ingramcontent.com/pod-product-compliance
Lightning Source LLC
Chambersburg PA
CBHW041608120626

46551CB00002B/350